SHADOW
SQUADRON

WHITE
NEEDLE

STONE ARCH BOOKS
a capstone imprint

A

Shadow Squadron is published by
Stone Arch Books,
A Capstone Imprint,
1710 Roe Crest Drive
North Mankato, MN 56003
www.capstonepub.com

Cataloging-in-Publication Data is available
on the Library of Congress website.

ISBN: 978-1-4342-6398-8 (library binding)
ISBN: 978-1-4342-6564-7 (paperback)

Summary: Syrian rebels have gotten
their hands on a White Needle, or stolen
chemical weapon, and plan to use it on an
unknown target. Only Shadow Squadron has
the talent and technology to locate and
neutralize the missile before it's launched.

Designed by Brann Garvey

Printed in China.
112014   008620R

CONTENTS

1316.981

2012.101

ACCESS GRANTED

CLASSIFIED

SHADOW SQUADRON DOSSIER

CROSS, RYAN

RANK: Lieutenant Commander
BRANCH: Navy Seal
PSYCH PROFILE: Cross is the team leader of Shadow Squadron. Control oriented and loyal, Cross insisted on hand-picking each member of his squad.

WALKER, ALONSO

RANK: Chief Petty Officer
BRANCH: Navy Seal
PSYCH PROFILE: Walker is Shadow Squadron's second-in-command. His combat experience, skepticism, and distrustful nature make him a good counter-balance to Cross's leadership.

YAMASHITA, KIMIYO

RANK: Lieutenant
BRANCH: Army Ranger
PSYCH PROFILE: The team's sniper is an expert marksman and a true stoic. It seems his emotions are as steady as his trigger finger.

BRIGHTON, EDGAR

RANK: Staff Sergeant
BRANCH: Air Force Combat Controller
PSYCH PROFILE: The team's technician and close-quarters-combat specialist is popular with his squadmates but often agitates his commanding officers.

JANNATI, ARAM

PHOTO NOT AVAILABLE

RANK: Second Lieutenant
BRANCH: Army Ranger
PSYCH PROFILE: Jannati serves as the team's linguist. His sharp eyes serve him well as a spotter, and he's usually paired with Yamashita on overwatch.

SHEPHERD, MARK

PHOTO NOT AVAILABLE

RANK: Lieutenant
BRANCH: Army (Green Beret)
PSYCH PROFILE: The heavy-weapons expert of the group, Shepherd's love of combat borders on unhealthy.

2019.681

CLASSIFIED

MISSION BRIEFING

OPERATION

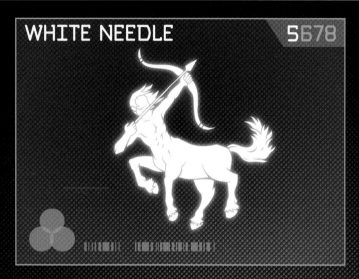

WHITE NEEDLE 5678

Syrian rebels have acquired a White Needle, or stolen chemical weapon. We already know they plan to use it, so it's our job to determine the target and prevent the launch. Two Israeli intelligence agents are willing to provide intel on the missing weapon in exchange for extraction from Syria. I'll be leading a team to rendezvous with them.

If we fail, gentlemen, it's likely that thousands of lives will be lost. I know we have the talent and technology to prevent that from happening. Let's get to it.

– Lieutenant Commander Ryan Cross

3245.98 ● ● ●

SYRIA

PRIMARY OBJECTIVE(S)

- Rendezvous with Israeli forces

- Recover missing chemical weapon

SECONDARY OBJECTIVE(S)

- Capture Syrian rebels responsible

- Limit enemy casualties

1932.789

0412.981

1624.054

DECRYPTING

12345

COM CHATTER

- CANALPHONE: an inside-the-ear two-way radio
- OVERWATCH: a small unit that provides tactics and intel from a good vantage point
- RECONNAISSANCE: the act of gathering intelligence
- UAV: UNMANNED AERIAL VEHICLE used to covertly gather intel

3245.98 ● ● ●

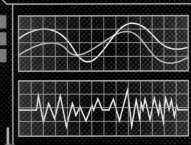

FRIENDLIES

Lieutenant Commander Ryan Cross led his four-man fireteam through the city of Al-Haffah, Syria. The center of the town lay ghostly and deserted. In the pale moonlight, the city's half-destroyed buildings loomed overhead like twisted fingers of dead giants trying to claw their way out from the earth.

"Lots of sniper holes, Commander," Lieutenant Kimiyo Yamashita informed Cross.

Yamashita was an experienced Army Ranger and the team's sniper, so Cross was inclined to take his word. Cross nodded. He directed the men to follow him closer to the cover of a ruined building nearby.

The town had been shelled by the Syrian army's artillery at the command of President Bashar al-Assad. He hoped to eradicate a group of rebels of the Free Syrian Army who had taken refuge there.

It was true that the overpowered rebels had fled to Turkey after the attacks, but Al-Haffah's battered landscape hardly looked like victory. To Lieutenant Commander Cross, the ruins suggested that Syria's president cared more about crushing the rebellion than he did protecting his people and their way of life.

The rebels of the Free Syrian Army would probably agree with Cross's opinion. In late 2010, much of Syria's citizenry had organized and carried out civil protests regarding the abuse of power by their government. The Syrian government responded violently to the protests, resulting in a civil war. While the United States, the United Nations, and other foreign entities would generally prefer to avoid interfering in civil conflict, President Assad's crackdown on rebels had been so brutal that the world couldn't stand by and do nothing.

The United States formally acknowledged the

rebels' Free Syrian Army (or FSA) as the true voice of the Syrian people. Nations on every border of Syria took in refugees who fled from the violence. A few allowed FSA rebels to hide on their soil while they regrouped and readied for the next battle.

For its part, the US considered itself invested in Syria's future. It had every reason to hope that the FSA would topple President Assad's ruthless regime. Hopefully, the Syrian government that arose from a rebel victory would take better care of its people's needs through a western democracy.

Aside from publicly voicing its support, the US government had taken no action to aid the rebels against their government. No weapons were donated, and no troops were deployed. To most of the world, America had taken no steps whatsoever.

Officially.

Unofficially, however, America involved itself in the Syrian conflict in one major way: It deployed Ryan Cross's Shadow Squadron.

Cross signaled toward a bombed-out house not far from the objective. "Take position there and get ready to give us some cover," Cross said to Yamashita, his voice barely a whisper. "In case we need it."

"Sir," Yamashita said.

The top-secret unit was comprised of elite soldiers from all branches of the military. It attracted only the best of the nation's soldiers and employed them on ultra-sensitive, top-secret missions — even missions they couldn't officially (or legally) be involved in. Therefore, while the US government claimed to have no official presence in Syria, it did have its best men on site to keep an eye on things.

The main US concern was that Syria's government possessed vast stockpiles of chemical weapons. The Syrian government had even begun moving them within the country as if they were preparing to use them.

If the government collapsed and if the rebels weren't able to restore order quickly enough, there was a real concern that some of the chemical warheads would fall into the wrong hands. Terrorists, criminals — any madman among them could cause destruction and chaos with those weapons.

Complicating things even further, certain terrorist organizations had taken an interest in helping the FSA against President Assad's government. Al-Nusra Front, or the Front for Victory of the People of Syria, had been committing reckless bombings and paramilitary attacks against the Syrian army since the beginning of 2012. Most of the FSA disapproved of their extreme tactics.

The idea of helping such criminals and terrorists was distasteful to the US, to say the least. However, the possibility that these same criminals and terrorists might gain access to Syria's chemical weapons arsenal in the event of a rebel victory was far worse. That was the real reason Cross's Shadow Squadron had been mobilized to Syria.

Based out of the neighboring and allied country of Jordan, the eight-man team conducted special reconnaissance and direct-action raids against locations in rebel-controlled Syria. Their goal was to limit Al-Nusra's extremist influence on the Syrian revolution. To that end, Shadow Squadron had been coordinating with special operators from Israel to monitor the location of Syria's chemical weapons. While they didn't work side-by-side with Israeli soldiers, they regularly traded information on persons of interest or chemical-weaponry parts.

One of these trades of information led Cross's fireteam to Al-Haffah early this morning. An agent of the Mossad — Israel's Intelligence Division — had arranged a trade of information that Cross was assigned to retrieve. Cross was used to being kept in the dark while infiltrating deep inside unfriendly territory, but he wasn't especially thrilled about it.

Cross turned to Second Lieutenant Aram Jannati, another Army Ranger. "I want you with Yamashita on overwatch," he said, handing over a tablet computer he'd been carrying.

"Sir," Jannati said, accepting the tactical pad from Cross.

With a tap on the screen, Jannati brought up a black-and-white image transmitted from the unmanned aerial vehicle (or UAV) hovering silently overhead. It had been following them ever since the fireteam set out. The UAV's low-light mini-camera provided a crisp, colorless image of the surrounding area. It showed no obvious sign of civilians or nearby hostiles.

Jannati turned the tablet screen toward Yamashita. "Where do you want to set up?" he asked.

"Here," Yamashita said after thinking for a moment. He tapped the image of a half-destroyed roof on a two-story house. It sat on a hill a block from their destination. Jannati nodded.

"Go," Cross said. He tapped the two-way canalphone nestled in his left ear. "High Road, this is Low Road. We need you to reposition Four-Eyes for us."

"Roger, this is Low Road," Staff Sergeant Edgar Brighton's voice replied in Cross's ear over the comm channel. Brighton was a technical genius and a Combat Controller from the US Air Force. He had designed the small quad-copter UAV, and now he piloted it remotely from where the rest of Shadow Squadron waited. "Just tell me where you want it."

Cross relayed new coordinates as Yamashita and Jannati relocated to their overwatch position. That left Cross alone with Hospital Corpsman Second Class

Kyle Williams, the team's medic. "Are we expecting to need cover out there, sir?" Williams asked.

"You know what I know," Cross said. "There shouldn't be anybody out there except for our contacts and maybe a few scavengers. Still, better to have cover and not need it than to need it and not have it."

"Fair enough," Williams said. "But what's so important we need to go pick it up in person?"

Cross shook his head. "Command wouldn't say. Either the Israelis didn't tell them or it's above our pay grade."

Williams tried to hide a frown, but Cross saw it. He felt the same way Williams did. In his experience, dealing with the Mossad was pretty much like dealing with the CIA. Both organizations tended to give out only as much information as it took to get soldiers like Cross and his men in trouble.

"In position," Jannati informed Cross a few moments later.

"Four-Eyes is ready too," Brighton reported.

"Route's clear to the objective," Jannati added. "We'll let you know if that changes."

Cross acknowledged the reports with a quick double-tap on his canalphone. Then he nodded to Williams, and the two-man team set out.

They crept slowly through the shadows cast by the twisted bones of the ruined neighborhood. They kept their M4 carbines at the ready, but they saw no signs of life except for a scrawny dog sniffing among some overturned trash cans.

KRAKA-BOOM!

BA-DOOM!

From far and near came the rumble of exploding bombs and the crackle of distant gunfire. Sneaking through the eerie ghost town, Cross realized how glad he was that his own country hadn't descended into modern-day civil war. It was the stuff of nightmares.

The rendezvous point was a house at the end of a cul-de-sac. It had escaped direct shelling and gunfire but had still been seriously damaged. At some point, a bomb had exploded near a car parked in the street, hurling the smashed vehicle into the front of the house like a knife. The wrecked car jutted upside-down from the wall by the front door.

"The back is clear," Jannati informed them over the canalphone.

Cross double-tapped his acknowledgement and led Williams around the back. No lights were on inside and no sounds came from within. Motioning Williams to take a position beside the rear door, Cross paused at the threshold. He gave three quick knocks.

NOK! NOK! NOK!

A moment later, a voice spoke from inside. "Jingle bells."

Cross gave a little smirk. "Batman smells," he answered, giving the agreed-upon password. Williams rolled his eyes.

"Wait," the inside voice said.

Cross heard a rattling of a makeshift barricade from inside. Then the door opened. A young Israeli in black fatigues held a sawed-off shotgun pointed at gut level. He looked Cross and Williams over with obvious confusion, noticing the lack of any identifying marks on their uniforms. "You're the Americans. Are you CIA?"

"Nope," Cross said. "Do you have some intel for us?"

"Inside," the Israeli said, backing off and lowering his shotgun. He disappeared into the house, prompting Cross and Williams to follow him. Williams closed the door behind them.

"I'm glad you made it," the Israeli soldier said. "Which one of you is the medic?"

"I am," Williams answered before Cross could stop him.

"Our orders didn't mention anything about a medic," Cross said. It was sheer chance that he'd picked Williams to accompany him to the house.

The Israeli sighed. "So this isn't a rescue?" he asked. He paused at the threshold of an interior room. "I should've known."

"What's your name? Are you hurt?" Williams asked. "Do you need a medic?"

"My name is Benjamin," the man said, "and I'm fine. It's Asher who's injured. He's been shot." He headed into a nearby room.

Williams pushed past Cross and hurried into the next room with the Israeli. On a cot lay a second Israeli, who'd been stripped to the waist and heavily bandaged around his stomach with cut-up bedsheets. Williams knelt at the man's bedside and slung off his pack. The first Israeli leaned against the wall and looked down at his wounded comrade with tired worry.

"Hey, Asher, can you hear me?" Williams asked. He lay one palm over the wounded man's forehead and took his pulse at the wrist with his other hand. The man lay immobile and unconscious. Sweat gleamed on his skin, and a dark bruise peeked above the topmost edge of the bandage. "He's burning up." He looked up at the first Israeli. "Where was he hit, Benjamin?"

"In his back," Benjamin said. "On the right."

"Commander, please give me a hand," Williams said.

Cross knelt beside Williams. Together they levered Asher onto his left side. At Williams' nod, Cross cut away the bandage until only a thick square of gauze remained over the wound site. Deep, purple-red bruises covered most of the wounded man's lower back.

"Hold that there," Williams said. "No exit wound. Severe bruising. Non-responsive. How long ago did this happen?"

Benjamin took a moment to realize Williams was speaking to him. "Huh? Oh, yesterday. What time is it?" He checked his watch. "Maybe 24 hours ago. A little longer."

Williams winced. "That's not good," he said. He dug through his medical pack and produced a set of fresh bandages.

"What happened?" Cross asked.

"Stupid, blind carelessness," Benjamin said. "We were in the mountains in Salma, monitoring a rebel cell. They were celebrating a victory and we were backing off to exfiltrate. We didn't realize they'd called up reinforcements to replace losses they'd taken. We blundered right into them, and they cut my team down. Asher and I got out and played *machboim* with them for a while until we found this place. They didn't seem too eager to follow us in here."

"Machboim?" Cross said.

"Hide and seek," Benjamin explained. "Anyway, when we got here I cleaned the wound and patched him up. I didn't think it was that bad at first. He just had a little bruising around the hole and very little bleeding. I thought we could wait for a rescue, but he's been getting worse all day."

"That's because he's bleeding internally," Williams said. He pressed stiff fingers hard into Asher's abdomen on the right side. The bruised flesh barely gave in at all. "See how rigid that is? His whole abdominal cavity is filling up with blood. He's got a high fever, which means he's got a severe infection. His pulse is weak and he's barely breathing. He's not reacting when I poke him like this. It should hurt like crazy, but he's not even twitching."

"Can you take the bullet out?" Benjamin asked, trying to stay calm. "Will that help?"

"Judging from where it went in," Williams said, "it's probably at least nicked his liver, his spleen, or his kidney. For all I know it's sitting inside one of those organs like a cork. It's a miracle he's lasted as long as he has."

"Is there anything you can do?" Benjamin asked. "Anything at all?"

Williams put on his most calm, blank, professional expression. Cross had seen it once before in the field — the day Second Lieutenant Neil Larssen had been killed in action during a covert op on an oil platform in the Gulf of Mexico.

"I'm sorry," Williams said. "It would've been unlikely even if you could've gotten him straight to a hospital."

Benjamin's face darkened. "His sisters will be devastated."

Cross backed off to give the Israeli a moment to feel his grief. He quietly tapped his canalphone. "High Road, this is Low Road," Cross said. "We need a pickup for two friendlies, one injured."

"Injured?" Brighton's voice replied in Cross's ear. "Who's —"

"Not one of ours," Cross said. "We're taking them back to base."

Cross double-tapped his canalphone to clear the channel. "Overwatch," he said, "reel in and get ready for pickup."

"Sir," Yamashita and Jannati replied.

Benjamin stood. "Where will you take us?" he asked Cross.

"Home," Cross said, "with a brief stopover at our base. We'll do everything we can for your man, I promise you that. But you'll owe us some information for the extraction."

"I'll tell you whatever you want to know," Benjamin said. He watched Williams finish re-bandaging his comrade's wounds.

When Williams was finished, Benjamin crouched in the medic's place. He placed his hand on Asher's chest and hung his head. Quietly and calmly, he murmured an Arabic prayer for the dead and dying over his comrade's body.

Cross walked over to Williams and stood beside him. "He's not going to make it?" Cross asked, barely above a whisper.

The medic shook his head. "He's lost too much blood, Commander," Williams said. "They're not going to be able to do anything for him back at base that I can't just do here."

"Such as?" Cross asked.

Williams let out a small sigh. "Load him up on morphine to ease his suffering," he said.

Cross grunted. "All right. Our ride back to base is going to be here in a few minutes. Get Asher ready to move, and ease his suffering as much as you can." He lowered his voice. "But save the morphine. We're not home safe yet, and one of our men might still need it."

"Yessir," Williams said. "I just hope whatever intel these guys found was worth it."

"Me too," Cross said.

INTEL

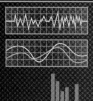

DECRYPTING
IIIIIIIIII   IIIIIIIIIIIIIIIIIII

12345

COM CHATTER

- EMPLACEMENT: a site used for artillery or weapons
- INTEL: intelligence, or information relevant to a mission
- SARIN: a potentially lethal nerve gas often used as a weapon

3245.98 ● ● ●

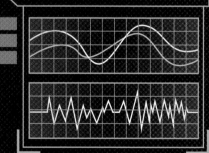

CHAPTER TWO

WHITE NEEDLE

1324.014

Several hours later, Shadow Squadron had returned to its temporary base in Jordan.

Asher, the wounded Mossad agent, had died in transport. The Americans put his body on a plane back home to Israel. The other agent, Benjamin, agreed to an intensive interview with Cross and Cross's superiors via two-way satellite broadcast. The intel Benjamin's team had gathered filled the gaps in information collected by Cross's team. All the data went to a crack team of analysts back at Command.

That analysis painted a terrifying picture. Cross called in the rest of Shadow Squadron for a briefing.

The team convened in the mess hall stuck onto the meager barracks they'd borrowed from the Jordanian army. Cross set up a palm-size projector on the end of the mess table and synced it to the tactical tablet computer he cradled in one arm.

Cross quickly glanced across the room to make sure everyone was present. He tapped his tablet's screen. The projector displayed an image on the wall beside him. Chief Walker shut the door and took a position on the opposite side of the projection.

Normally Cross preferred Walker to sit with the men during a mission briefing, but this time he didn't mind the extra support up front.

"Well this can't be good news," Brighton whispered to Yamashita. "Walker and Cross aren't even glaring at each other."

Yamashita ignored him.

"We have a serious problem," Cross said. "An emergency interrupt just came down from Command. We're going mobile in one hour for a White Needle emergency."

Eyes widened on every face in the room. White Needle was code for a rogue chemical weapon and implied that it was in the hands of an enemy with intent to use it.

"Give them the background, Chief," Cross said, handing the tablet over to Walker. "The short version."

"Sir," Walker said, taking the tablet. He swiped away the first image to replace it with a dossier photo of an olive-skinned, bearded man in his late 50s. "You all remember our target, Abdul-mateen Shenwari. He's an Afghani mujahedeen who was behind bombings and raids in Afghanistan, Yemen, and Iraq. Intel confirms that he's up to more of the same stuff in Syria. He's organizing and helping supply cells of FSA fighters against President Assad's army."

Nods and low murmurs went around the room. Shadow Squadron had originally been tracking Shenwari in Iraq, but a rash of bad intel had allowed the criminal terrorist to slip through their fingers. When CIA informants declared that Shenwari had resurfaced in Syria, Cross's team had been reassigned there to aid in ongoing operations. But Shenwari always remained one step ahead and just out of reach.

"The intel our Israeli friend provided helped us identify the top two locals working under Shenwari here in Syria," Walker said. He advanced the image on the tactical pad, breaking out two more dossier photos beneath Shenwari's photo. Both photos were taken secretly, as neither man seemed aware of the fact that he was being photographed. Both photos showed lean, hard-faced young Syrian men.

"The first one is Baltasar Dyab," Cross explained. "He's commanding a raid on an artillery emplacement overlooking the mountain town of Salma in the Latakia Governorate."

Walker nodded, then tapped the tactical pad. A map of the northwestern coast of Syria appeared. The towns of Salma and Latakia were highlighted on the map.

"The Syrian Army's been raining shells and missiles on the city of Salma for months," Walker said. "So the rebels taking control of the emplacement is a pretty important local victory."

Walker advanced the image on the screen once more. A picture of Shenwari's other local lieutenant appeared. "Our Israeli friend was also able to confirm something we'd suspected but hadn't been able to prove," Walker said. "Last week, FSA rebels ambushed a supply convoy en route from Latakia. We knew that Shenwari's other top local man was behind the raid, but we didn't know much more than that. Now we do. The convoy was en route from a chemical munitions facility in the city, moving sarin gas to a secondary location. We thought the convoy and all its materiel had been destroyed, but Mossad's information indicates that the FSA actually made off with a large amount of sarin gas. Enough for a single warhead."

"How long have they known about this?" Yamashita asked with a scowl. "Surely not since before the raid."

"We believe they did," Cross said grimly.

"They knew this last week? And they're only just

telling us now?" Brighton asked. "What the heck were they waiting for?"

"They might not have told us anything at all if we hadn't extracted their men from Al-Haffah," Jannati said.

"That wasn't a favor," Yamashita said. "They knew their men needed extraction. They just *called* it an 'information drop.'"

"Didn't they think we'd help if they just asked?" Brighton asked. "I don't know if that's devious or lazy or —"

"But where's the connection?" Staff Sergeant Paxton asked, cutting in. "Between the convoy ambush and Salma, I mean."

Cross took the tactical pad back from Walker. He gave Paxton a grateful nod for getting things back on track. "All available evidence suggests that Shenwari has ordered his two lieutenants to regroup their separate forces in Salma with the sarin gas," Cross said. "Hence our White Needle emergency. Our own intel indicates that they are planning to arm and launch a chemical warhead from the artillery position the FSA just captured. And signs point to sooner rather than later, before Assad's army can take back control of that emplacement."

"What's the range of their warhead from that position?" Paxton asked.

Cross swiped across his tactical pad and brought up a map of western Syria. The towns of Salma and Latakia were surrounded by a progression of rings that expanded out into the neighboring cities, as well as into Turkey to the north. Centers of high population density within those rings were all marked on the map, as well as important Syrian Army military bases and Turkish refugee camps to the North.

"As you can see," Cross said, "their range of attack is alarmingly large."

"How do we know they're planning to use what they have?" Sergeant Shepherd asked. "I don't see how it would benefit them. The western world is already on their side. Everybody's worried President Assad is going to use these things on his own civilians. What could the rebels gain from using the warhead?"

"It's Shenwari we're worried about," Cross said. "He's radical and unstable and dedicated to his jihadi cause. If he's got a weapon like this, he will use it — it's just a matter of time. Fortunately, our intelligence is ahead of the curve for once, and we've got a chance to stop him."

Cross placed his hands on his desk and leaned forward. "So we're heading to Salma to neutralize Shenwari's chemical weapon capacity," he said. "If we can recover the weapon or weapons, great. If not, we're authorized to destroy them. As a secondary objective, we're to kill or capture Shenwari if he's at the site. If not, we're to scoop up one or both of his lieutenants for questioning."

"Sounds simple enough," Yamashita said. "Are we coordinating with the Israelis on this?"

Cross and Walker both shook their heads. Cross kept his expression blank, but Walker's face betrayed some of the frustration both men felt.

"The Israelis are staying out of this one," Cross said tightly. "They say they've already lost too many men putting the puzzle pieces together for us."

Cross swiped and tapped on his tablet screen to bring up low-light camera footage taken from a high vantage point. It showed recent imagery of the Syrian Army's artillery emplacement in the mountains near Salma. It wasn't much to see, but it did give a decent idea of the emplacement's layout and size.

"That's footage from the Avenger UAV," Brighton offered.

"Correct," Cross said with a nod, clearly impressed that Brighton could identify the UAV solely by its photos. "It was taken a week ago — before the raid. We're trying to get a UAV or a satellite over the area to provide fresher intel, but this is the best we can do at the moment."

Cross paused to produce a laser pointer from his hip pocket. He shined it on the southern portion of the map. "We'll be inserting via Wraith from this direction..."

INTEL

DECRYPTING
|||||||| ||||||||||||||

12345

COM CHATTER

- AVENGER: a UAV, or unmanned aerial vehicle, used remotely for reconnaissance

- FROG-7: Soviet missile launcher

- LZ: landing zone, or where a helicopter touches down

- WRAITH: stealth helicopter

3245.98 ● ● ●

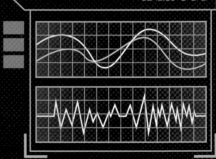

CHAPTER THREE

WRAITH

Within the hour, the team was in the air, aboard its Wraith stealth helicopter. A heavily modified Sikorsky Blackhawk, the Wraith used state-of-the-art scythe-shaped rotors, a radar-deflecting surface, and a host of other top-secret innovations. It was almost impossible to see in the night sky, detect on radar, or even hear unless it was right overhead. The muffled engine noise and reduced propeller turbulence made for an eerie stillness inside the passenger compartment, except for a strange humming sound. Cross had ridden in the Wraith plenty of times, but the unnerving hum still got under his skin.

"Go over the safety briefing again, Williams," Cross said. "Humor me."

"Sir," Williams half-said, half-sighed. He leaned forward on his bench seat. "The chemical in our White Needle is sarin. It's clear, odorless, and tasteless. You can be exposed through your skin, your eyes, or through respiration. It's heavier than air, so if it gets loose, it's going to roll right downhill."

"Right toward us," Brighton said. His insect-like, panoramic night-vision mask sat atop his head, leaving his expression clearly visible. Although he had a smile on his face, it looked sickly and strained.

"Yes," Williams said. "And it acts fast, so you're going to have to watch yourselves and each other for symptoms."

"And if you do notice symptoms," Cross added, "tell me immediately so we can get out of the area."

"Right," Williams said. "The signs to watch out for are: runny nose, watery eyes, drooling, sweating, headache, blurred vision, eye pain, cough, chest tightness, confusion, weakness, nausea…"

Cross nodded and let Williams trail off. What Williams didn't point out was that those symptoms indicated a relatively mild exposure to sarin. Higher concentrations of the deadly chemical would result in convulsions, paralysis, loss of consciousness, and respiratory failure — all within just a few seconds. There would be nothing Williams could do for them so it was best not to fill their heads with fear.

"Just out of curiosity, Commander," Brighton asked, "why aren't we doing this mission in full-on rubber chemical suits?"

None of Cross's men had voiced this question before now. Apparently, they trusted that their commanding officer had a compelling reason.

"For one thing," Cross said, "the odds of us coming in contact with actual sarin gas are minimal. The components Shenwari's locals stole are binary. They remain separate and harmless until the warhead mechanism mixes them into sarin in flight. If they do launch it via missile, we're not the ones who are going to have to worry about the gas."

Brighton and the others nodded. Apparently

the explanation set their minds at ease, even if it shouldn't have.

"Second," Cross continued, "this artillery emplacement is up in the coastal mountains, and we're going to be inserting downslope via Wraith to preserve the element of surprise. That means we're going to goat-foot it upslope, and take it from me — you do not want to do that in a full chemical suit. The lighter we travel, the faster we move, the sooner we get the job done."

"All right, Commander," Brighton said. "That makes sense." He paused for a moment then turned to Williams. "But you're stocked up on whatever the antidote for sarin is, right?"

"I'm stocked up on atropine sulfate and diazepam," Williams said, patting his first-aid kit. Cross knew that wasn't exactly the cure that Williams made it out to be.

"He can also provide you one lollipop if you don't cry too much," Shepherd said, grinning, as he dug an elbow into Brighton's ribs.

Williams chuckled. "They're sugar-free," he said.

"Blech," Brighton said, sticking out his tongue. "I'd rather have the sarin."

"Quiet down," Cross said over the laughter. "We're just a couple minutes out from the LZ. Get squared away. It's almost time."

"Sir," the men murmured. Their faces turned hard and serious. Cross was glad for the break in the tension — he could always count on Staff Sergeant Brighton to provide one — but this was no longer time for jokes.

* * *

When the Wraith reached its destination, it paused high above the artillery emplacement occupied by FSA rebels, possibly commanded by Abdul-mateen Shenwari.

"Bird's eye is coming online now, Commander Cross," the helicopter pilot said through Cross's canalphone.

"Roger that," Cross said. "We're syncing up with you now."

Brighton made a few taps and swipes on the

tablet computer he held in his lap. A live feed from the helicopter's powerful fiber-optic cameras came on line. It wasn't as good as the feed would have been from Brighton's own Four-Eyes, but high winds over the mountains had forced them to leave his UAV behind. As the image became clear, Brighton looked up at Cross and gave him a thumb's up.

"We have a visual," Cross said. "Stand by to take us to the landing zone."

"Roger that," the helicopter pilot said. "Approaching the LZ."

"Huddle up," Cross said, half-joking. The interior compartment of the Wraith was hardly spacious when packed full of eight soldiers and their gear. Cross motioned for Brighton to hand him the tablet. He positioned it so all the men could see it.

Cross switched the overhead camera footage into a wide-angle view of the terrain. He overlaid it with contour lines showing the area's relative elevation. The overtaken Syrian artillery emplacement was little more than a flat, rocky ridge at the top of a gently sloping path. A flimsy wooden cabin had been erected there at some point, likely to provide sleeping quarters for the artillery crew, but it had since been surrounded by tents. Three M116 75mm pack howitzers stood at the ready by the edge of the ridge. A flatbed truck that had likely transported the weapons was visible next to the tents. FSA rebels hung around the howitzers, but they didn't appear to be tending the weapons or preparing to operate them. There was no sign of ammunition for the weapons.

Between the howitzers and the nearby mortars was another truck. It was this one that drew Cross's attention: the boxy, eight-wheeled brick of a vehicle with a long, steel rail structure on top. A crane apparatus reached down over one side. Beside the truck, being lifted by the crane, was a 30-foot-long steel missile. The missile was a 9K52 Luna-M, more commonly referred to as a FROG-7. It had an effective range of 70 to 90 kilometers and could travel at a top speed of three times the speed of sound. In other words, the target would never hear it coming.

Most importantly, the FROG-7 was capable of launching a chemical warhead. And from what Cross could tell, the men clustering around the FROG-7 were preparing to deliver just such a warhead to some unsuspecting target. When the men in the Wraith realized this, they let out a collective gasp.

"Okay, then," Cross said. He tapped his canalphone to include the Wraith's pilot in what he had to say. "Guys, plan one is out. They're getting ready to launch down there, so we're escalating this to a full-court press. Our main objective is to disable that missile — and anybody who tries to get anywhere near it."

"I'm packing two Hellfire missiles, Commander," the Wraith pilot informed him. "I can blast that launcher apart from up here, if you like."

"The Hellfires don't burn hot enough," Cross said. "I can't risk a detonation throwing liquid sarin all down the mountainside and into the city of Salma."

"I suppose that's a fair point, Commander," the pilot said, his voice full of disappointment. "Negative on the Hellfires."

Cross smirked. "Actually, go ahead and put one into those howitzers," he said. "They should be far enough from the FROG-7 to minimize the danger."

"I can do that," the pilot said excitedly.

"After that I want a quick sweep with the miniguns across the open ground. Then get us down and let us out. Fast. You can hop back up here when we're clear."

"You got it," the pilot said.

"Guy sure seems to like his artillery," Brighton joked.

"I heard that," the pilot said.

"Chief Walker," Cross said, "I want you, Shepherd, Brighton, and Jannati out of the Wraith and down first. Yamashita and I will cover you, then you sweep us clear a space to follow you. When we're down, we'll make for the FROG-7 and eliminate the surrounding resistance. Once it's ours, Brighton will disarm and disengage the FROG-7's warhead. Then we hold position until the Wraith comes back and gets us outta there."

"Sounds simple enough," Chief Walker said sarcastically.

Cross didn't blame him. He knew that as soon

as he gave the order, all hell was going to break loose, and his simple, straightforward backup plan would be an exercise in barely constrained chaos. Fortunately, his men had surprise on their side.

"All right," Cross said. "Every man knows what he needs to do?"

The men of the Shadow Squadron nodded. "Roger that," the Wraith's pilot said through the canalphone.

Cross's heart rate sped up. The sour and cold taste of surging adrenaline made his lips peel back in a wild, involuntary grin.

"Let's do it," he said.

INTEL

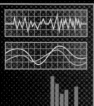

DECRYPTING
||||||||| ||||||||||||| ||||

12345

COM CHATTER

- HELLFIRE: air-to-surface missile
- HOWITZER: high-trajectory, high-power artillery
- M4 CARBINE: short and light automatic assault rifle
- TRACER ROUNDS: used in bullet magazines to track direction of gunfire

3245.98 ● ● ●

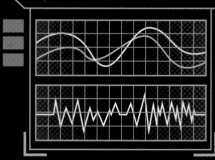

CHAPTER FOUR

FROG-7

The Wraith descended in a wide, spiraling arc, its nose pointed down toward the rocky ridge. Recessed panels on the Wraith's underside folded open, revealing two Hellfire missiles. At the pilot's click of a switch, one of the missiles lanced down into the cluster of unmanned pack howitzers.

KA-BOOOOM!

The howitzers exploded in a blaze of heat and thunder. Their twisted wreckage flew off the ridge and down the mountainside.

The pilot spun the Wraith in midair and launched the second (and last) Hellfire missile into the cluster of mortars on the other side of the emplacement.

WIRRRRRSH!

The smaller, lighter mortars disappeared in a cloud of billowing smoke and earth. There was no wreckage left behind. The vehicles parked near the mortars were damaged beyond repair, as well.

The pilot's assault couldn't have caused more confusion and activity. Rebels dashed out of their tents and out of the cabin and began running in all directions. With their weapons drawn, they tried and failed to find the source of the attack. To clarify the situation for them, the pilot made his presence more than obvious by opening fire with a pair of M-134 miniguns.

RAT-A-TAT-TAT!

RAT-A-TAT-TAT!

The miniguns laid down two tight streams of 7.62x51mm NATO rounds at a rate of nearly 50 rounds per second. The sun-bright lines of tracer rounds and the vicious power of the regular rounds scattered the soldiers, though not all of them were able to get to safety.

All the while, the Wraith descended toward the side of the emplacement that was farthest from the mountain road. When the chopper reached a safe height, it opened its doors and dropped a pair of rappelling ropes from each side. Walker, Shepherd, Brighton, and Jannati were already clipped onto the ropes to descend. Cross and Yamashita stepped forward and knelt in the opening next to the others.

"Go!" Cross ordered.

The first four-man fireteam stepped out of the Wraith and slid quickly down their ropes. Cross and Yamashita provided covering fire with their M4 carbines, picking off those few fighters below who had stood their ground and fired up at the helicopter. The two best shots in Shadow Squadron, Cross and Yamashita easily kept their fellow soldiers safe all the way to the ground.

The four men below unclipped themselves from the lines and formed up to move toward the FROG-7 launcher.

"Ready up!" Cross ordered. Then he, Williams, Yamashita, and Paxton clipped onto the ropes and dropped out of the Wraith to join their comrades.

As Cross's group slid down, those already on the ground took a knee and laid down suppressing fire. Walker and Jannati fired in three-round bursts from their M4 carbines. Brighton let loose with more intimidating and less precise blasts from his AA-12 combat shotgun, chewing up the side of the cabin where some of the gunmen had taken cover.

The most effective cover fire came from Shepherd. He tucked his M240 machine gun under one arm like a madman and swept it in an arc across the area.

RAT–A–TAT–TAT!

RAT–A–TAT–TAT!

It was a terrible firing position for a belt-fed machine gun, but it was undeniably effective at backing off the enemy force.

"To the FROG-7!" Cross said as his second team touched down and unclipped from the rappelling lines. A high-speed winch slurped the lines back up into the Wraith, and the helicopter disappeared into the night sky.

Brighton pointed toward the wreckage where the mortars and the rebels' parking lot had been. "RPG!" he shouted. The team turned to see a man with a rocket-propelled grenade launcher aimed at the Wraith.

Cross and Yamashita both fired a round with their M4s. Their target jerked and fell, firing just as his legs went out from under him. A line of white smoke shot upward through the air, missing the Wraith by mere yards.

"Yikes!" the pilot yelped in Cross's canalphone. "Thanks, fellas!"

"All clear, Wraith," Cross and Yamashita replied. They glanced at each other and cracked a quick grin.

"Go!" Cross ordered.

As one, Shadow Squadron rushed across the emplacement, dodging fire from the few FSA fighters who'd taken cover.

Shepherd kept the shooters pinned down with machine gun fire as he and Paxton brought up the rear. Unfortunately, a group of FSA soldiers had taken cover by the FROG-7, which Cross didn't realize until his men were right up on it. Two men popped out from behind the heavy truck to open up with AK-47s.

BANG! BANG!

BANG! BANG!

Brighton managed to nail one of them with a thunderous blast from his AA-12, throwing the man back against one of the launcher's tires. The other squeezed his rifle's trigger, spraying automatic fire.

POP-POP-POP!

POP-POP-POP!

The rounds hit Walker, Jannati, and Williams before a three-round burst from Cross cut the second gunman down. Walker was hit in the lower leg. Jannati caught two bullets in his ballistic vest. The last shot punched through Williams' upper right arm, missing his chest by less than an inch. Walker and Williams both cursed roughly. Jannati would have done the same if the shots hadn't knocked the wind out of him.

Cross ordered his team to establish a defensive perimeter and to secure the FROG-7 and its loader. Shepherd and Paxton took a position behind a line of waist-high rocks. They set up the M240 machine gun and opened up with it. Yamashita knelt beside them and added his deadly single-shot cover fire to Shepherd's more manic automatic fire. As the FSA fighters' return fire turned erratic, Paxton popped up and hurled an M67 frag grenade into the wooden cabin.

BOOOOOOOOM!

The explosion rattled the structure and blew out its last remaining window. He threw a second grenade into the nest of ruined vehicles where most of the FSA rebels had taken refuge.

BA-ROOOOM!

In the wake of the second detonation, the return fire ceased. Murmuring voices and the whimpers of the wounded could be heard in the darkness, but no one seemed too eager to engage Shadow Squadron anymore.

While Shepherd, Paxton, and Yamashita were doing their work, the other five members of the team had their hands full securing the FROG-7. The rebels had finished loading the missile onto its launcher before Shadow Squadron had touched ground, and a team of tenacious gunmen had holed up around the machine to defend it. Two of those fighters had surprised the squad and wounded Williams and

Walker. At least two more men remained alive on the opposite side of the launcher.

As Williams helped Walker hobble over to the launcher, Brighton rushed over to them and helped Williams break out his first-aid kit. Jannati, meanwhile, shook his head clear and gulped down a deep, ragged breath. He'd found himself taking a knee next to the body of the man Brighton had shot. The body belonged to Sargon Balhous — one of Abdul-mateen Shenwari's top local lieutenants.

When Jannati had his breathing under control, Cross motioned for him to get up and move with him. Cross then motioned for Brighton to stay with Williams to aid and cover the medic while he tended to the injuries. Brighton gave a quick nod and hefted his AA-12 at the ready.

Cross led Jannati to the corner of the launcher and paused at the edge to listen. He heard two voices conversing in Arabic in desperate, rushed whispers. Cross heard the click-clacking of a computer keyboard and was able to make out the words "coordinates" and the Arabic phrase "Allahu yaghefiru liy."

Cross signaled for Jannati to follow him, then he vaulted over the high bumper of the FROG-7 truck and sprang around the corner at a high angle. Jannati came around a second later at ground level. The two FSA fighters on that side of the truck were ready for some sort of attack, but Cross's unconventional tactic caught them off-guard.

BANG!

The quicker of the two FSA men fired where Cross's chest should have been. Instead the shot hit only the empty air between his knees.

BANG!

BANG!

Cross shot the soldier in the shoulder and Jannati emerged a second later to finish him off. The second man was crouched over a mobile data terminal that was plugged into the side of the FROG-7 truck. Cross's second shot missed him by inches.

The man—none other than Shenwari's other local lieutenant, Baltasar Dyab — mashed one last key on the data terminal.

CLICK!

He looked up at Cross and Jannati with an expression of hopelessness. Tears gleamed in his eyes as he spread his hands and backed away from the keyboard.

Jannati raised his rifle and growled, "What did you —"

KIRRRRRRSSSSH!

A moment later, the roar of the FROG-7's rocket answered Jannati's question. Heat, pressure, and an unbelievable roar obliterated the capacity for rational thought. Cross and Jannati could only watch helplessly as a 30-foot-long missile loaded with sarin gas roared upward into the night.

INTEL

DECRYPTING
||||||||| ||||||||||||| |||||

12345

COM CHATTER

- HUD: heads-up display, or the visual overlay on a computer screen
- PATRIOT MISSILE: the MIM-104 is a surface-to-air weapon
- STINGER MISSILE: a portable, surface-to-air weapon
- ZIP-CUFF: a lightweight version of handcuffs

3245.98 ● ● ●

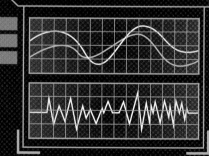

AVENGER

"Allahu yaghefiru liy," Dyab murmured. He was staring at the ground as the missile accelerated into the sky. He repeated the phrase over and over again.

Jannati raised his weapon to shoot the man down, but Cross raised a hand to stop him.

"Balhous is dead," Cross said. "We need this one alive if we're going to find Shenwari."

Jannati scowled. "Fine. I'll wrap him up." He ordered Dyab to lie down on his stomach and put his hands behind his back. The FSA fighter did so without complaining. He just kept muttering "Allahu yaghefiru liy" over and over as Jannati bound his wrists with a zip-cuff from his pocket.

"Brighton, get over here!" Cross yelled.

Brighton had already come around the truck. He snapped his wraparound night-vision system up over his head. His eyes were saucer-wide.

"The rocket's up," Cross said, his voice flat but strained. "Can you—"

"Where's it headed?" Brighton asked. "I mean, Israel and Damascus are that way." He pointed south. "Turkey's that way." He pointed north. "And... well, nothing's west of here but the ocean."

"It's going into Saraqeb," Baltasar Dyab interrupted. "Allahu yaghefiru liy."

"Saraqeb's rebel-held, you idiot!" Jannati snapped, tightening the zip-cuffs on his prisoner's wrists.

"Can you stop it?" Cross asked Brighton. "Blow it up, turn it around, or something?"

"Not from here, man," Brighton said. "The FROG-7's not a guided missile. This launcher's not a remote control. It's just a big truck with a rail on top. That's all."

"What can stop it?" Cross said. "The Wraith?"

"The Wraith won't be able to catch it," Brighton said. "Do we have any Patriot missiles nearby?"

Cross shook his head.

"Then I don't know," Brighton said, looking sick. "How about a miracle? Anybody owe you one of those?"

Cross grabbed Brighton by the shoulders and held him face to face. "People are going to die, Sergeant. They're counting on you. I'm counting on you. There must be something you can do!"

Brighton looked terrified. Cross forced himself to take a deep breath. He was only making things worse, and they were rapidly running out of time. If that warhead was heading for Saraqeb, they only had a few minutes to do something about it.

"Ed," Cross said slowly and calmly. "You can do this. If anybody can solve this problem, you can. So work it out. What do you need to get that missile out of the air? Nothing's off the table. Just name it and I'll make it happen.."

Brighton closed his eyes and took a deep breath. He thought hard for what seemed an eternity of precious seconds. Then his eyes flew open. "Where's the Avenger?"

Cross felt a glimmer of hope. The Avenger was a modified General Atomics MQ-1 Predator Drone. It had high-quality cameras, a powerful engine, radar-deflecting stealth fuselage, and an array of air-to-air and air-to-surface missiles. Only the CIA and the Joint Special Operations Command knew it even existed.

"It's over Aleppo," Cross said, his excitement growing alongside Brighton's. "Is that close enough?" Aleppo, the largest city in Syria, was only 25 miles from Saraqeb.

"It'll be tight," Brighton said. "Get it moving toward us, then get me control of it. I'll bring that missile down."

"Command," Cross barked, opening the emergency channel over his canalphone. "I need a hotlink feed from the Avenger's camera to my team's tactical pad and a secure line to Colonel Max Gordon in Colorado."

As Cross began sorting things out through channels, Brighton took the tactical pad out and plugged it into the truck's mobile data terminal. When he had them linked up, his fingers flew over the keyboard. Soon he had established a connection via satellite link to the US Air Force base back in Colorado where the top-secret Avenger unmanned aircraft was remotely piloted. He accepted the Command-approved feed from the Predator's cameras, but he hit a brick wall when he tried to access the drone's flight controls.

"I can't get in!" he cried. Hacking a top-secret Air Force command center with the equipment he had on hand wasn't realistic.

"Gordon, listen to me!" Cross was saying to the man on the other end of the comm channel. "I don't have time for this. This is a White Needle emergency and a Shadow-tier mission. Your people don't have security clearance for this. Just get us access to that UAV. Now!"

After a moment, Cross nodded. He looked at Brighton. "Okay, he needs to know our—"

"Just make him tell Lieutenant Wallace in their Security Department to stop fighting me," Brighton interrupted. "I can do the rest from here."

Cross relayed the information, then he moved to stand behind Brighton. The moment Colonel Gordon complied and allowed Brighton access to the Avenger's flight controls, Brighton stood up straight. He held the tactical pad out in front of him in both hands like a car steering wheel. The screen showed a front-facing camera view along with a complicated HUD that Cross could barely decipher.

"Got it!" Brighton said. "Interface is up, tablet's synced… And holy crap, I'm flying the Avenger!"

Cross marveled at what Brighton had been able to accomplish in less than a minute. By tilting and turning the tactical tablet, he was able to control the pitch, yaw, and roll of the Avenger UAV. Through an interface on the touchscreen, he also had control of acceleration and the weapons system. The interface was crude, but it was good enough for the problem at hand. Brighton oriented the tablet, aiming the armed drone in the right direction. Then he opened the accelerator all the way up. Cross watched in amazement as the Avenger streaked westward from the Aleppo Governorate tearing across the sky toward Saraqeb.

"Won't take more than a minute, Commander," Brighton said.

"That's all the time we've got," Cross said. He stepped away from Brighton to check on the rest of his men. Jannati had led Dyab around to the other side of the launcher truck, where Williams was just finishing directing Walker in how to properly bandage the bullet wound in Williams' arm. A heavy bandage already shone white around Walker's calf.

"Report," Cross said.

"Area secure, sir," Walker said. It was ostensibly good news, but Walker's expression was clouded by a faint scowl. All along, Walker had made no secret of the fact that he wasn't happy having to potentially shoot and kill FSA rebels, even in the name of a greater good. "The rebels have all bugged out. The ones left alive, anyway."

"Good." Cross gave a whistle at the small covering fireteam of Yamashita, Shepherd, and Paxton. "Hey, guys, reel in. Get hands under these two and get ready for evacuation." He turned back to Walker. "Call the Wraith back in."

"Sir."

Cross came back around the truck to find Brighton staring hard at the tactical tablet. His fingers were white-knuckled from gripping too hard.

"All right, breathe, Sergeant," Cross said peeking over Brighton's shoulder. At some point, Brighton had switched the display to a thermal readout. The pinpoints of stars were gone from the night sky, and the city heat of Saraqeb glowed like plankton on the sea's surface. And in the center of the screen was a white-hot point of heat: the FROG-7 rocket.

"Is that it?" Cross asked. "Take it down."

"It's not close enough yet, Commander," Brighton said through clenched teeth. "Give me a second. Just give me a second..."

Cross watched the screen over Brighton's

shoulder, feeling just as tense as Brighton was. The rocket began to tilt downward, and Brighton tilted the tablet ever so slightly to cause the Avenger UAV to match it. Long, painful seconds went by, allowing the rocket to grow larger on the display. The lights of Saraqeb began to take up more and more of the screen.

"Brighton..." Cross urged.

"There!" Brighton shouted.

TAP!

Brighton jammed his thumb down on the weapons overlay on the UAV's heads-up display, launching the Avenger's full complement of air-to-air Stinger missiles. Glowing streaks of fire filled the screen. They rapidly closed in on the FROG-7 rocket. Brighton and Cross held their breaths as the missiles closed in on their target...

...and missed.

"What?" Brighton yelped. "No way!"

"Tell me you've got more of those," Cross said, fighting to keep the sudden fear out of his voice. "Sergeant?"

"Everything else is air-to-ground," Brighton said with a shrug. "I'd never hit that tiny little thing. But there's one thing left I can try."

"Whatever it is, do it," Cross said.

"I'm already on it, Commander," Brighton said. "Just one quick question: how much did the Avenger cost?"

Cross was about to unleash his rage at what seemed to be another of Brighton's smart-aleck remarks. Then Cross realized what Brighton was getting at as he watched him maneuver the Avenger down below the oncoming rocket.

Cross moaned. "Twelve to fifteen million dollars," he said, defeated. "Do it."

"My condolences to their budgeting department," Brighton said. He pitched sharply back and upward. When the FROG-7 reappeared on the Avenger's camera display, it took up almost the entire screen.

FZZZZZZZZZZT!

The feed from the Avenger disappeared. Brighton had crashed the UAV into the rocket, destroying both devices harmlessly high above the Saraqeb skyline.

Brighton lowered the tactical tablet and looked up at Cross. His shocked, adrenaline-flared expression was an exact match for the way Cross felt.

But when Brighton finally spoke, it was in a small, hushed voice. "I ain't paying for that, by the way."

"Me neither," Cross said just as quietly.

* * *

The Wraith carried Shadow Squadron and its prisoner back to the temporary base in Jordan. Dyab remained silent. Even when Cross told him that Brighton had destroyed the rocket and its entire chemical payload with no loss of life, the FSA lieutenant didn't even look up from his lap.

Cross glared down at Baltasar Dyab. "Why did you launch the rocket at Saraqeb?" he demanded.

Now the man did raise his eyes, but they were blank and hopeless.

"Answer him!" Jannati barked, shoving Dyab from behind with the sole of his boot. He clutched his chest where the bullet had hit his vest.

"Why Saraqeb?" Cross asked again, with a quick scowl at Jannati to calm the man down. "It's still under FSA control. Why target there?"

"Shenwari," the prisoner answered. "He convinced us it was a worthy sacrifice."

"Worthy?" Jannati snapped. "Thirty-thousand people live in Saraqeb! Rebels and innocent civilians..."

"Martyrs," Dyab said, his tone hollow. "He said they would be rewarded in Heaven and that Syria would be free."

Jannati was practically beside himself. Words failed him. Cross thought he understood what the Syrian meant, but he left it up to Walker to explain — which Walker had already taken the initiative to do.

"You weren't going to claim responsibility, right?" Walker said. "You were going to leave that position as soon as the rocket was away. That way, the entire world would think it was Assad's men who fired it on your people."

"Yes," Dyab said. "And then the rest of you, watching but never involving yourselves, then you would have to help us. That's what Shenwari said. Only he said you would reveal your true colors to the world by failing to help us. You would make excuses and —"

"Don't try to make this about us," Cross said. "It's not about us. It's not even about Shenwari, though he deserves some of the blame here. The fact of the matter is, the horror we stopped here tonight is all on you. You, Baltasar. You were the one who launched the rocket. You were the one who could've said no, but you didn't."

Dyab broke eye contact and hung his head. Whether he believed Cross or agreed with him, he gave no sign.

"Allahu yaghefiru liy," Dyab murmured,

retreating into his own internal world once more. "May God forgive me."

"We'll see," Cross told him. "We'll see."

MISSION DEBRIEFING

OPERATION

WHITE NEEDLE

5678

PRIMARY OBJECTIVES

- Rendezvous with Israeli forces

- Recover missing chemical weapon

SECONDARY OBJECTIVES

- Capture Syrian rebels responsible

x Limit enemy casualties

STATUS

3/4 COMPLETE

3245.98

CROSS, RYAN

RANK: Lieutenant Commander
BRANCH: Navy Seal
PSYCH PROFILE: Team leader of Shadow Squadron. Control oriented and loyal, Cross insisted on hand-picking each member of his squad.

Talk about a close call -- and an expensive one. I'm just thankful that Brighton was able to save the day. These things really need to stop coming down to the wire, though -- my heart can't handle it.

I'm going to have to make this debriefing, well, brief since Command is on my case regarding operational expenses for this mission. Apparently "it was our only option" isn't a sufficient excuse for destroying a multi-million-dollar UAV. But I'll be sleeping well at night knowing how many lives we saved.

– Lieutenant Commander Ryan Cross

2019.681

CREATOR BIO(S)

AUTHOR

CARL BOWEN

Carl Bowen is a father, husband, and writer living in Lawrenceville, Georgia. He was born in Louisiana, lived briefly in England, and was raised in Georgia where he went to school. He has published a handful of novels, short stories, and comics. For Stone Arch Books, he has retold *20,000 Leagues Under the Sea*, *The Strange Case of Dr. Jekyll and Mr. Hyde*, *The Jungle Book*, *Aladdin and the Magic Lamp*, *Julius Caesar*, and *The Murders in the Rue Morgue*. He is the original author of *BMX Breakthrough* as well as the Shadow Squadron series.

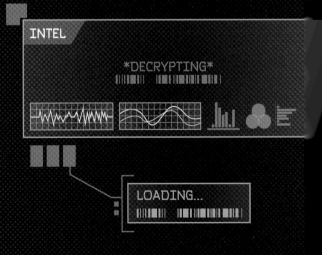

INTEL

DECRYPTING

LOADING...

ARTIST

WILSON TORTOSA

Wilson "Wunan" Tortosa is a Filipino comic book artist best known for his work on *Tomb Raider* and the American relaunch of *Battle of the Planets* for Top Cow Productions. Wilson attended Philippine Cultural High School, then went on to the University of Santo Tomas where he graduated with a Bachelor's Degree in Fine Arts, majoring in Advertising.

ARTIST

BENNY FUENTES

Benny Fuentes lives in Villahermosa, Tabasco, in Mexico, where the temperature is just as hot as the sauce. He studied graphic design in college, but now he works as a full-time illustrator in the comic book and graphic novel industry for companies like Marvel, DC Comics, and Top Cow Productions. He shares his home with two crazy cats, Chelo and Kitty, who act like they own the place.

2019.681

AUTHOR DEBRIEFING

ACCESS GRANTED

CARL BOWEN

Q/When and why did you decide to become a writer?

A/I've enjoyed writing ever since I was in elementary school. I wrote as much as I could, hoping to become the next Lloyd Alexander or Stephen King, but I didn't sell my first story until I was in college. It had been a long wait, but the day I saw my story in print was one of the best days of my life.

Q/What made you decide to write *Shadow Squadron*?

A/As a kid, my heroes were always brave knights or noble loners who fought because it was their duty, not for fame or glory. I think the special ops soldiers of the US military embody those ideals. Their jobs are difficult and often thankless, so I wanted to show how cool their jobs are and also express my gratitude for our brave warriors.

Q/What inspires you to write?

A/My biggest inspiration is my family. My wife's love and support lifts me up when this job seems too hard to keep going. My son is another big inspiration.

He's three years old, and I want him to read my books and feel the same way I did when I read my favorite books as a kid. And if he happens to grow up to become an elite soldier in the US military, that would be pretty awesome, too.

Q/Describe what it was like to write these books.
A/The only military experience I have is a year I spent in the Army ROTC. It gave me a great respect for the military and its soldiers, but I quickly realized I would have made a pretty awful soldier. I recently got to test out a friend's arsenal of firearms, including a combat shotgun, an AR-15 rifle, and a Barrett M82 sniper rifle. We got to blow apart an old fax machine.

Q/What is your favorite book, movie, and game?
A/My favorite book of all time is *Don Quixote*. It's crazy and it makes me laugh. My favorite movie is either *Casablanca* or *Double Indemnity*, old black-and-white movies made before I was born. My favorite game, hands down, is *Skyrim*, in which you play a heroic dragonslayer. But not even *Skyrim* can keep me from writing more *Shadow Squadron* stories, so you won't have to wait long to read more about Ryan Cross and his team. That's a promise.

COM CHATTER

-MISSION PREVIEW: After an unknown aircraft crashes in Antarctica near a science facility, Shadow Squadron is deployed to recover the device. But when Russian special forces intervene, Cross gets caught between the mission's objective and the civilian scientists' safety.

3245.98 ● ● ●

SHADOW SQUADRON

PHANTOM SUN

CARL BOWEN

PHANTOM SUN

Cross tapped his touchscreen to start the video. On the screen, a few geologists began pointing and waving frantically. The camera watched them all for another couple of seconds then lurched around in a half circle and tilted skyward. Blurry clouds wavered in and out of focus for a second before the cameraman found what the others had pointing at — a lance of white fire in the sky. The image focused, showing what appeared to be a meteorite with a trailing white plume behind it punching through a hole in the clouds. The camera zoomed out to allow the cameraman to better track the object's progress through the sky.

"Is that a meteorite?" Shepherd asked.

"Just keep watching," Brighton said, breathless with anticipation.

Right on cue, the supposed meteorite suddenly flared white, then changed directions in mid-flight by almost 45 degrees. Grunts and hisses of surprise filled the room.

"So… not a meteorite," Shepherd muttered.

The members of Shadow Squadron watched in awe as the falling object changed direction once again with another flare and then pitched downward. The camera angle twisted overhead and then lowered to track its earthward trajectory from below.

"And now… sonic boom," Brighton said.

The camera image shook violently for a second as the compression wave from the falling object broke the speed of sound and as the accompanying burst shook the cameraman's hands. A moment later, the object streaked into the distance and disappeared into the rolling hills of ice and snow. The video footage ended a few moments later with a still image of the

gawking geologists looking as excited as a bunch of kids on Christmas morning.

"This video popped up on the Internet a few hours ago," Cross began. "It's already starting to go viral."

"What is it?" Second Lieutenant Aram Jannati said. Jannati, the team's newest member, came from the Marine Special Operations Regiment. "I can't imagine we'd get involved if it was just a meteor."

"Meteorite," Staff Sergeant Adam Paxton corrected. "If it gets through the atmosphere to the ground, it's a meteorite."

"That wasn't a meteorite, man," Brighton said, hopping out of his chair. He dug his smartphone out of a cargo pocket and came around the table toward the front of the room. He laid his phone on the touchscreen Cross had used, and then synced up the two devices. With that done, he used his phone as a remote control to run the video backward to the first time the object had changed directions. He used a slider to move the timer back and forth, showing the object's fairly sharp angle of deflection through the sky.

"Meteorites can't change directions like this," Brighton said. "This is 45 degrees of deflection at least, and the thing barely even slows down."

"I'm seeing a flare when it turns," Paxton said. "Meteors hold a lot of frozen water when they're in space, and it expands when it reaches the atmosphere. If those gases are venting or exploding, couldn't that cause a change of direction?"

"Not this sharply," Brighton said before Cross could reply. "Besides, if you look at this…" He used a few swipes across his phone to pause the video and zoom in on the flying object. At the new resolution, a dark, oblong shape was visible inside a wreath of fire. He then advanced through the first and second changes of direction and tracked it a few seconds forward before pausing again. "See?"

A room full of shrugs and uncomprehending looks met Brighton's eager gaze.

"It's the same size!" Brighton said, tossing his hands up in mock frustration. "If this thing had exploded twice — with enough force to push something this big in a different direction both times — it would be in

a million pieces. So those aren't explosions. They're thrusters or ramjets or something."

"Which makes this what?" Shepherd asked. "A UFO?"

"Sure," Paxton answered in a mocking tone. "It's unidentified, it's flying, and it's surely an object. It probably has little green men inside, too."

"You don't know that it doesn't," Brighton said. "I mean, this thing could be from outer space!"

"Sit down, Sergeant," Chief Walker said.

Brighton reluctantly did so, pocketing his phone.

"Don't get ahead of yourself, Ed," Cross said, retaking control of the briefing. "Phantom Cell analysts have authenticated the video and concluded that this thing isn't just a meteorite. It's some kind of metal construct, though they can't make out specifics from the quality of the video. I suppose it's possible it's from outer space, but it's much more likely it's man-made. All we know for sure is that it's not American made. Therefore, our mission is to get out to where it came down, secure it, zip it up, and bring it back for a full analysis. Any questions so far?"

"I have one," Jannati said. "What is Phantom Cell?"

Cross nodded. Jannati was the newest member of the team, and as such he wasn't as familiar with all the various secret programs. "Phantom Cell is a parallel program to ours," Cross explained. "But their focus is on psy-ops, cyberwarfare, and research and development."

Jannati nodded. "Geeks, in other words," he said. Brighton gave him a sour look but said nothing.

"What are we supposed to do about the scientists who found this thing?" Lieutenant Kimiyo Yamashita asked. True to his stoic nature, the sniper had finished his breakfast and coffee while everyone else was talking excitedly. "Do they know we're coming?"

"That's the problem," Cross said, frowning. "We haven't heard a peep out of them since this video appeared online. Attempts at contacting them have gone unanswered. Last anyone heard, the geologists who made the video were going to try to find the point of impact where this object came down. We have no idea whether they found it or not, or what happened to them."

"Isn't this how the movie Aliens started?" Brighton asked. "With a space colony suddenly cutting off communication after a UFO crash landing?"

Paxton rolled his eyes. "Lost Aspen, the base there, is pretty new," he said. "And it's in the middle of Antarctica. It could just be a simple technical failure."

"You have zero imagination, man," Brighton said. "You're going to be the first one the monster eats. Well... after me, anyway."

"These are our orders," Cross continued as if he had never been interrupted. "Find what crashed, bring the object back for study, figure out why the research station stopped communicating, and make sure the civilians are safe. Stealth is going to be of paramount importance on this one. Nobody has any territorial claims on Marie Byrd Land, but no country is supposed to be sending troops on missions anywhere in Antarctica, either."

"Are we expecting anyone else to be breaking that rule while we are, Commander?" Yamashita asked.

"It's possible," Cross said. "If this object is man-made, whoever made it is probably going to come looking for it. Any other government that attached the same significance to the video that ours did could send people, too. No specific intel has been confirmed yet, but it's only a matter of time before someone takes an active interest."

"Seems like the longer the video's out there, the more likely we're going to have company," Yamashita said.

"About that," Cross said with a mischievous smile on his face. "Phantom Cell's running a psy-ops campaign in support of our efforts. They're simultaneously spreading the word that the video's a hoax and doing their best to stop it from spreading and to remove it from circulation."

"Good luck to them on that last one," Brighton snorted. "It's the Internet. Phantom Cell's good, but nobody's that good."

"Not our concern," Cross said. "We ship out in one hour. Get your gear on the Commando. We'll go over more mission specifics during the flight. Understood?"

"Sir," the men responded in unison. At a nod from Cross, they rose and gathered up the remains of their breakfast. As they left the briefing room, Walker remained behind. He gulped down the last of his coffee before standing up.

"Brighton's sure excited," Walker said.

"I knew he would be," Cross replied. "I didn't expect him to try to help out so much with the briefing, though."

"Is that what I'm like whenever I chip in from up here?" Walker asked.

Cross fought off the immediate urge to toy with his second-in-command, though he couldn't stop the mischievous smile from coming back. "Maybe a little bit," he said.

Walker returned Cross's grin. "Then I wholeheartedly apologize."

SEA DEMON

CARL BOWEN

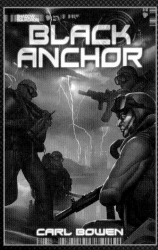

BLACK ANCHOR

CARL BOWEN

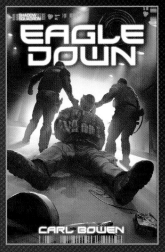

EAGLE DOWN

CARL BOWEN

SNIPER SHIELD

CARL BOWEN

SAVING...

2012.101

2012.101